Johns Hopkins: Poetry and Fiction
John T. Irwin, General Editor

BREAK DOWN LANE

Poems by

Robert Phillips

The Johns Hopkins University Press
Baltimore and London

© 1994 Robert Phillips
All rights reserved
Printed in the United States of America on acid-free
paper
03 02 01 00 99 98 97 96 95 94   5 4 3 2 1

The Johns Hopkins University Press
2715 North Charles Street
Baltimore, Maryland 21218-4319
The Johns Hopkins Press Ltd., London

Library of Congress Cataloging-in-Publication Data
will be found at the end of this book.
A catalog record for this book is available from the
British Library.

ISBN 0-8018-4854-7
ISBN 0-8018-4855-5 (pbk.)

For Elinor P. Cubbage,
Sister & Poet

I write out of my experience not about it.
John Ashbery

Poetry is a revelation of language
rather than of personality.
Robert Duncan

Contents

EROSIONS

By age forty we all have
the face we deserve,
someone wrote. Do I deserve
mine at fifty-three?
Start with the nose—
bulbous, red as Clarabel's;
doubtless too many Dewars.
That's no cure for depression.

Regard the broken veins
roadmapping the cheeks.
"Gin blossoms" W. C. Fields
called his. They wended
so floridly across his face,
no amount of pancake makeup
could hide them from
the camera's inquiring eye.

Speaking of eyes, mine are
slits—little red pig eyes.
The scar by the sinister one,
souvenir of a Christmas
when I was young. Up before others,
in the dark I tripped,
bashed my face directly
across the cast-iron platform

of a gift rocking horse.
Blood would not stop until
Doc drove in three clamps.
The other scar, below that?
Reminder of a chance encounter
with a mugger in a men's room.
He beat me, threatened to "snuff"
me if I called out for help.

Some say I am lucky. I say why
do I still perpetuate teenage
acne in middle age? What
should I do not to lose
fistfuls of hair when I shampoo?
How can I stop skin cancer,

burnt and gouged out of my fore-
head regularly as the solstice?

How can I arrest erosion
in my brow, furrows visible
as the canals on Mars?
Auden's description of his face:
"A wedding cake left out in the rain."
My brow competes with Auden's,
worry lines deepening by debts,
non-paying tenants, legal suits.

Why do all three chins sag?
This A.M. I managed a fresh
glance into the looking-glass.
I saw the face buried within
my face. It is my father's,
my grandfather's, bland, plain
as a pudding. Yet some
say they were handsome men.

Whereabouts

(for Richard Howard)

Isn't it odd how anyone who disappeared
        is said to have been sighted in San Francisco?
What is it about that city with its steep
        streets that so inclines them?

Consider Judge Crater, snapped by Polaroid
    weeding on his knees in his San Mateo garden.
Or the Brach candy heiress after a quake,
        stuffing currency into a sidewalk crevice,

generous to a fault. Ambrose Bierce is seen
        and heard rehearsing his *Devil's Dictionary*
in a Chinese take-out joint on Grant.
        And that boy with bangs pushing crack

and his buns in Haight-Ashbury? Etan Patz,
        no longer young, eyes cunning and feral.
Jimmy Hoffa, set deep in the cement
        of his ways, emerges from the Sheraton-Palace,

a floozie on each arm. He's come a long way
        from Detroit. And wasn't that Amelia Earhart
boarding the Red Eye at International,
        wearing only one size 9 Cat's Paw shoe?

There's Dick Diver strap-hanging on a cable car,
        Michael Rockefeller atop the Transamerica,
Weldon Kees still contemplating San Francisco Bay,
        '52 Ford on the approach ramp. He never left.

Don't they know we need them all to stay away?
        Our mythology's poor enough even without them.
They must remain precisely as last seen,
        just before fadeout, their famous last scene.

Easy Street

It is always several blocks away,
around a corner, a corner
you probably never will turn.

The people who live there seem ordinary
enough, but richer, their houses
and cars bigger, newer, unfinanced.

Every backyard sports a swimming pool.
The people who live there seem
to sleep just like you and me,

but it is a different kind of sleep,
untroubled by dreams of failed exams,
automobiles skidding out of control.

Their children—there are perfect children—
never complain of having to clean
plates of paté de foie gras and filet.

Uniformed maids waltz about bearing
feather dusters, but there never is
any dust. Drains do not clog there,

furnaces never fail. Ladies
of the house wear white satin
just like Jean Harlow, spend hours

on white telephones. Their dogs wear
diamond collars, sleep in dog houses
with conditioned air. Lap cats lap

saucers of heavy cream from Limoges.
The men of course never go to work.
They play the links and clip hedges

against inflation. Hulking as elephants,
armored trucks make home deliveries
of more money. If you ever move there,

lock all your windows and doors.
Everyone wants the same address.
Some will simply kill to get it.

*. . . he loves the world so much he wants to steal
and eat it.*—Jarrell on Picasso

Making off with it wasn't difficult,
just a giant green apple spinning.

No one kept guard. He reached out,
plucked it, and ran like holy hell.

He hid behind a bush, took a bite.
He thought he'd swallowed Africa whole—

the taste, dark as eggplant. Next bite,
fruity yet dry—unmistakably France.

But the next, plain as porridge!
England or Ireland or the Orkneys.

He turned it around, bit in again.
It was smoky Southwest barbecue.

Then Russia, salty and fishy as caviar,
more than he could chew. Next course

he encountered China—not Cantonese,
but jalapeño hot and spicy. It took

all of Iceland to cool his mouth.
Australia? Dry and moldy as old sneakers.

To clear the palate, a sweet dessert
of floating Caribbean islands.

Now it's gone. He consumed it all.
Who can say he isn't worth it?

His work will be nourished by it.
And when his inspiration wanes,

he'll turn his attention elsewhere—
to Venus, Uranus, the stars.

On a Drawing by Glen Baxter

For a few years, I managed to eke out
        a meagre living as the Human Yo-Yo.
But I tired of the unnatural activity,

arms folded, legs tucked, head bent,
        going toward the sod like a Duncan Imperial
(those expensive blockheads). Once oriented,

you cannot imagine the effort to reverse direction,
        rotating still, sometimes fighting
nausea, straining to rewind, to rewend

my way back. My act was revolutionary,
        but it made my head spin. And he who sent me
reeling took glee in casting me out faster

each time—wham, WHAM, WHAMMO!—until I thought
        my spine would snap. It's hard on the neck,
too. Oh, the tricks he made me do!

Mastering Cat's Cradle was not easy,
        intricate string designs while suspended
in midair. How humiliating to perform

Walk the Dog down on my knees!
        (He even made me wear a spiked collar
and bark ferociously.) But

the last straw, he urged me to perform
        Around the World. I told him to bugger off.
Now I hear he's latched onto a model

who Glows in the Dark. Befitting one
        so unenlightened. As for me, I'm employed
in a bar as a Dwarf Tossee. I'm small enough,

nearly. I wear helmet, knee and elbow pads,
        the wall is Velcro, so is my suit.
If they're not too drunk and toss me right,

I stick, don't feel a thing, hardly.
        What the hell. After the Human Yo-Yo,
it's an act of downright upward mobility.

1.
The thing of it was,
you looked so handsome
and trustworthy—
such a nice smile.

The thing of it was,
you showed me
a laminated ID card,
said you were Police.

The thing was, you see,
I was seventeen,
didn't know people
could buy fake IDs.

Thing of it was,
you told me someone
had been arrested
breaking into my car,

did I want to go
down to the station
and press charges?
You'd drive me.

You had a hot car,
smooth, brand new.
Smelled like leather,
a turn-on. Like you.

2.
Not far down the road
you pulled over,
quickly handcuffed me,
unzipped yourself,

started waving a pistol.
You said you'd blow
my brains all over
the highway if I didn't

do what I was told.
Whatever the reason, I didn't
think you would.
(Your cock was tiny,

soft as a slug.) Somehow
I got the door open,
ran. You didn't fire,
but came after me

waving a tire jack.
I wore high heels,
couldn't run fast.
Thought I was a goner.

Then a VW came along.
I lifted my handcuffed
hands and hollered.
It stopped for me.

3.
I'm one of the lucky few.
I've seen your picture
in all the newspapers.
No question, it was you.

I've seen your face
most nights in dreams,
big as the harvest moon,
grinning like a goon.

It's the good-looking
ones I distrust most—
the way they try to
sweet-talk their way.

Last week in a bar
a guy walked over,
touched my shoulder.
In the ladies' room

I puked my guts out.
I'll find one so homely

someday, I'll simply
go along with him. Okay?

Fifteen years after,
you finally got fried.
Clean-shaven bastard,
inside me you're still alive.

On Finding a Former Lover
Cut All Dedications to Me
from Her Selected Poems

Opening your imposing *oeuvre*,
I search for my name appended
as previously to certain early
anthology pieces. Instead,

nothing; dedications deleted,
expunged, exterminated vermin.
Sweetiepie, I marvel how you
rewrite your (and our) past,

as if I'd never labored to make
certain stolid poems lithe.
("Litheness is all," we agreed.)
My name belongs with those

like ham belongs with eggs,
fireworks with Fourth of July.
Your late poems? Just ham,
no fireworks, cellulite anti-

climaxes of the facelift years.
I marvel at your reworking
personal history, as I marvel
at your persistence in remarrying:

Have you yet learned to count
to ten? May your current husband
awake to discover his vital member—
like certain dedications—excised.

I thought it was just a righthand
lane where traffic that has
to drive slow goes,

or a lane where you can halt, curse,
trip on blinker lights,
and wait for a tow.

Yet here I find myself limping along
in the breakdown lane.
No car, no motorcycle,

just me in my sad sneakers, painfully
gaining no more than three
miles an hour,

an out-of-shape marathon man to whom
no spectator passes Gatorade,
wheezing like a Hoover,

taking in landscapes on each side,
the mathematical precision
of August cornrows,

the clean lines of suburban houses
armored in aluminum siding.
Motorists that flow

past on the left are totally in control.
I thought I saw my successful
brother streak by

steering a Lexus. My wife drifted
by on a float. Evening-gowned,
she's Miss Congeniality.

Father drove a steamroller by, flattening
all wildlife that strayed
in his path.

I'm sure my hated office rival gave me
the finger from an open Porsche.
What really hurt

was when my younger self hot-rodded by,
confident, and never acknowledged
me. No one stops,

I don't want them to, it's my breakdown,
I earned it, I'll just stagger
toward the horizon, not

knowing what's ahead, whether there is
a finish line, or why I am crying
on the shoulder.

The Married Man

(for Judith Bloomingdale)

I was cut in two.
Two halves separated
cleanly between the eyes.
Half a nose and mouth on one
side, ditto on the other.
The split opened my chest
like a chrysalis, a part
neat in the hair.
Some guillotine slammed
through skull, neck, cage,
spine, pelvis, behind—
like a butcher splits
a chicken breast.

I never knew which side my heart
was on. Half of me sat happy
in a chair, stared at the other
lying sad on the floor. Half wanted
to live in clover, half to breathe
the city air. One longed to live
Onassis-like, one aspired to poverty.
The split was red and raw.

I waited for someone to unite me.
My mother couldn't do it. She claimed
the sissy side and dressed it like a doll.
My father couldn't do it. He glared
at both sides and didn't see a one.
My teachers couldn't do it. They stuck
a gold star on one forehead,
dunce-capped the other.

So the two halves lived in a funnyhouse,
glared at one another through the seasons;
one crowed obscenities past midnight,
the other sat still, empty as a cup.
One's eye roadmapped red from tears,
the other's, clear and water-bright.
Stupid halves of me! They couldn't even
decide between meat and fish on Fridays.
Then one began to die. It turned gray as old veal.

Until you entered the room
of my life. You took the hand of one
and the hand of the other
and clasped them in the hands of you.
The two of me and the one of you
joined hands and danced about the room,
and you said, "You've *got* to pull yourself
together," and I did, and we are two-
stepping out lives together still,

and it is only when I study hard
the looking-glass I see that one
eye is slightly high, one corner
of my mouth twitches—a fish on a hook—
whenever you abandon me.

AN AFFAIR
WITH
THE MUSE

Hardwood

With a shudder and a pop and a crack,
    a celebration startles me awake.
I rush into the living room. The dead
    fireplace log is all ablaze in the dark.
What had been cold white char now is dancing
    behind the screen, David before the Ark.

That's the way this hardwood life has been, holding
    its smolder deep inside for an age,
waiting to burst out into flame again.
    Until you came like Abishag one night,
I'd chilled to the thought of a second life.
    Unlike David, I rekindle, burn bright.

The Embodiment

How will I ever write a poem for you,
          who are the embodiment of a poem—
a work tourists would stand in line to see
          at some Fascist-picketed museum
in Italy? That old virtuoso,
          Bernini, certainly would see the light
which is within you, delight in shaping
          your superior form into stone, as
he turned frozen Daphne into a tree.
          But frozen's not what you were meant to be
to me. Your walk has feet like prosody.
          As you enter a room, I come aware—
the shudder of the hound scenting the hare.
          How will I ever write a poem for you?

We went to hear the famous pianist.
     I wanted to sit on the left, to watch
his hands. You preferred the right, to observe
     his face. I was after facile technique,
you the shifting ranges of emotion.
     I yielded, we camped on the right. His face—
bland tapioca pudding—came alive,
     reflected adagios, prestissimos!
And that piano, Bösendorfer grand,
     on its raised and mirrored lid, made a show
of his hands: As in the best of affairs,
     my surrender was none. By giving in,
     I got what I needed.

Sun-streamed afternoons
your apartment is flooded

like the Grand Canal,
the room a chiaroscuro.

Vermicular shadows slide
the walls. Like Venice,

we are suspended in time,
the only movement a drift

of motes, we two adrift
within a vermeil glow.

There is no winged lion,
no muscular gondolier,

but a consolation, church
bells in an empty piazza.

You never mind so much sun.
When you draw the Venetian

blinds, I take it as sign
you want to make love. Segue

into dark, the interior
of the Basilica of St. Mark.

The doves outside flutter
into this single mass.

To wake up with you
      curled like a possum in bed:
Don't stir for hours.

As you lie sleeping,
      I study your sculptured face,
those acute hip bones.

The hair on your head
      is curly as pubic hair,
just as edible.

The birds arouse you,
      the birds the bluejays have robbed
of sunflower seed.

Or perhaps squirrels,
      whom I defend. But you say,
"Rats with bushy tails!"

Late last night, my dear,
      you yourself were bushy-tailed—
Potter's Squirrel Nutkin.

The birds arouse you,
      so I reach and do the same.
In bed, morning dew.

The two of us wet,
      we stride from bed,
sunrise in Eden.

There are too many birds here.
Their singing drives me to distraction,
awakens me at uncivilized hours.

At dusk, peepers—do you know what they are?—
do their quaint thing throughout
the cocktail hour. I could go mad.

Too many tall pines surround this cabin.
They drop shabby brown needles everywhere
and keep the sun from ever coming in.

Too many wildflowers litter the fields.
They think being pretty's enough. It's not.
And seeing one deer is one too many

when missing company of another sort.
So how are things in the hot big city?
You could have answered just one of my letters.

Terminal

When I enter Grand Central Terminal now,
I look up at the Balcony Cafe, see you
seated at the yuppie bar where we used
to meet Friday nights to compare weeks.
My heart sticks like an electric fan
that won't oscillate. Only then I see
it isn't you. It's someone else—less
attractive, more abundantly available.

Nothing is quite what it seems any more.
Love, you don't linger in the station
waiting, don't take the Local to the town
where you and I were a couple to those
who knew us by sight, by sound. Your heart
commutes to a different station now,
mine's an auto stalled across the tracks
while the Metro Express roars in, fast.

Everyone has his price, the saying goes,
and so has every thing. That tag sale
where we browsed an afternoon away
showed us the value of what we underrate—
garden tools, hat racks, empty picture frames.

We fell in love with a matched pair
of Jacobean chairs: tall backs, knobby legs,
soft leather of otherworldly blue. Neither
of us had room for two. We each took one home,
like a pickup from a singles bar.

Mine's in the den, yours the living room.
Mine's used every evening, yours pines away
unfulfilled. You think it's a mistake.
And now we never see each other any more.
The matched pair wonders why they were split up.

The cat sits in the windowseat
alert for squirrels and for birds.

She will not listen to my explanation
that the mulberry tree was cut down.

She will not pay me any nevermind
when I say those who came for berries—

greedy as winter—took their hunger
somewhere else. No. She sits, sinews

poised, eyes surveying the astonished
landscape, and waits, and waits,

expectant as the white telephone
on the nearby writing desk.

She will not comprehend an absence
of berries and of lively tree,

anymore than I will comprehend
the five weeks since your last call.

As a top slows, teeters, falls on its side,
vacation stalls to a halt. Rain six days
running, newspapers limp, sand underfoot,
kids frantic—too young for Trivial Pursuit.

TV's broken. The multi-movie house
had something new, but rain drew the tourists:
I circled for miles, there was just no way
to park. Back again, she takes up macrame.

I undertake the unnecessary: shave again,
sort hardware I don't even own.
Cocktails at five, too much looked forward to.
Phone-boothed one night, I call my old flame.

The inadequate mattress receives the blame
for dreams I comprehend in the morning.
My bearded boss fires me without warning.
I drop the ball, lose the JV game.

I want to see us walk through spring again,
through Old Bedford, our bodies and backgrounds
so different, you impressed by mansions,
I proud to share a world you never knew.

I want to study your profile again,
secretly, in the darkened movie house
where we've come to see some dumb comedy,
I want to eat warm popcorn, touch your breast.

I want to hear again the rain tapping,
sliding your windowpanes, stroking your door,
gargling in your gutters while we're drinking
tea and memory. That's how it should be.

Today a bluejay and I own my backyard.
The lilac blossoms have burnt themselves out.
Yet the air's awash with honeysuckle.
The azalea bursts its heart out.

Despair

It blooms in white rooms
after fluorescent lights come on.

It sighs in the air conditioning
of Holiday Inns.

It dashes a foot against a rock
where there is no rock.

It worries at the annual convocation
of the Optimists' Club.

It builds dungeons in spring air.
It is a duck dead on the pond.

It is a heart lost on Valentine's Day.
It lives on the dark side of the moon.

It turns one face to the wall.
It is a coupon which is irredeemable.

It is the incurable disease,
the blight, the empty mailbox,

the composite of Job's comforters.
It is my smile, which you misconstrue.

The one to whom I always felt most close
died, and I could never comprehend why
I felt no loss, no grief, shed not one tear.
I kept her picture close by, a souvenir
of times past, foreign, even a bit quaint.
And years went by and still I felt that way
until one night, a party, she was there
(this was in a dream, but more real than real).
More beautiful than she had been in life,
dressed to the nines, she mingled, made small talk,
and eventually came over to me:
"I've been missing you, every single day,"
she said. My tears released, she went away.

The Stone Crab: A Love Poem

Joe's serves approximately 1000 pounds of crab claws
each day.—*Florida Gold Coast Leisure Guide*

Delicacy of warm Florida waters,
his body is undesirable. One giant claw
is his claim to fame, and we claim it,

more than once. Meat sweeter than lobster,
less dear than his life, when grown that claw
is lifted, broken off at the joint.

Mutilated, the crustacean is thrown back
into the water, back upon his own resources.
One of nature's rarities, he replaces

an entire appendage as you or I
grow a nail. (No one asks how he survives
that crabby sea with just one claw;

two-fisted menaces real as night-
mares, ten-tentacled nights cold
as fright.) In time he grows another,

large, meaty, magnificent as the first.
And one astonished day, *snap!* it too
is twigged off, the cripple dropped

back into treachery. Unlike a twig,
it sprouts again. How many losses
can he endure? Well,

his shell is hard, the sea is wide.
Something vital broken off, he doesn't
nurse the wound; develops something new.

WINDLESS
TIMES

It's dead as a rail spike, they say.
They even pulled up all the ties
from Wilmington to Virginia. Not even a freight
can get from here anymore. Don't listen to such lies.

A certain kind of train still gets through.
The one that took young Tommy Waller
north to summer camp, Silver Lake, organized
sports. That season he grew three inches taller.

Or the train that brings Grand Mary south,
her annual visit—Grand Mary in the latest fashions,
red fox furs, hennaed hair, matching alligator luggage,
in the Parlor Car sipping Manhattans;

her favorite grandchild, I was mesmerized
by her talk of the Stock Market, famous friends,
horse races, the Stork Club, Broadway . . .
I'm as old now as she was then.

But that's the sort of passenger train gets through.
The one bringing Private First-Class Jack Studley home
from Manila, lots of medals and him still in one piece.
He's met by Mom and Dad and Janet Lee Jones,

whom he will marry. You can't stop a train
like that. Or the one bearing LaVerne Purdy's
body. She ran off to Hollywood to become a star,
came home in a pine box, not yet thirty.

Then there's the train carrying the President, his wife.
It stopped on a side rail. We were under his spell
while he spoke. Pre-TV, this was our only glimpse.
We liked him. "Give 'em hell, Harry!" we yelled.

That kind still comes through. They're dirty,
brass unpolished, prickly plush seat cushions
explode dust clouds when you sit down. But
the conductor waves at me when the engine rushes

by, and Laddie—my collie then—runs parallel
to the cars till the train is halfway to Hebron.

Some even say old Mister Register, the telegraph operator,
is holed up inside the boarded-up train station.

His ghostly tappa-tappa-tap electrifies windless times,
recreates signals that don't seem to signify anymore.
Listen! I think I hear the eleven-thirty-four!

At the back of our property
        was a sandpit we called The Hole.
Soldiers, it was our Pork Chop Hill.
        Cowboys and Indians, our butte.

In those pre-Canaveral days,
        it never became a crater
of the moon, or we astronauts.
        It was a place to hide for hours.

Some first discovered sex down there,
        genitals rubbed through corduroy.
Every autumn when we raked leaves,
        we'd dump the bushel baskets down,

bushel upon bushel building
        orange and yellow immensities.
And our discarded Christmas trees
        were tossed to the furthermost side.

Nothing but clean fill was left there.
        We'd level that hole before long,
we thought, but we never came close.
        It's still a hole, choking on weeds

and poison ivy, ice and snow.
        It is the pit I never fill
which I feel sometimes when I hear
        a train split the town late at night,

a stray dog bark at the bitch moon,
        a screen door slam a world away.

The Ride

(In memorium: T.A.P.)

In my dream the Ferris Wheel went around
        and Christmas tree lights were strung far below.
Each time the wheel stopped the seats rocked and rocked.
        I was the last to be let off. But no,

the wheel started to turn again and pitched
        itself in a whirlwindish pace,
twirly and swirly like Sambo's tigers!
        Myself seven, alone, wind in my face.

"Stop this thing, I want to get off and go
        to bed," I wanted to stand, shout aloud.
But there was no way my voice could be heard,
        and standing up simply was not allowed.

Next I noticed the crowd began to leave,
        concessions closing, kiddie rides shut down.
Colored lights were extinguished here and there.
        I'd be abandoned! I felt my heart pound.

Then I saw a big man—I knew who
        he was, though he was just silhouette.
He wandered to the levers, yanked down hard.
        The wheel began to slow its pirouette.

Seat by seat I approached solid ground.
        Finally it stopped, I got out. A moment
later he put an arm around my cold shoulder.
        In silence my father and I drove home.

"The man of the family always carves,"
Mother rehearsed, cutting deeply into the rib roast.
She cast glances toward Father, who hunched
at the head of the table in the tallest chair,
Irish linen napkin tucked into the neck of his plaid
shirt. He claimed not to know how to carve.
     His smile was weak as water.

"My father was an exquisite carver,"
she announced to assembled guests, or just to us
four kids waiting for interminable Sunday dinner
to end, Ed Sullivan's "Toast of the Town" to begin.
"He had a way with joints," she reminisced, trimming
away all fat, slices falling one after another
     like a stack of dominoes.

"He could carve a ham paper thin.
If you held a slice to the light, you could see
clear through!" We children sniggered. Why would
anyone hold meat to the light? Why would how thin
it was make any difference in how it tastes?
She sawed away like a virtuoso cellist. Finally
     the knife struck bone.

"He was also a connoisseur of wine,
drove the finest horse and carriage in all Roanoke.
But I have always thought the true measure of a man
was how well he could carve." With that she lay
aside the ancestral carving knife, bestowed
a generous portion onto a Wedgwood plate, and passed
     Father the choicest cut.

Walnuts

After she died, Father chainsawed the walnut
    tree down. Unharvested nuts leave too much mess
upon the blackened, frozen ground. Till then,
    every year, walnuts fell in the backyard,
recalcitrant ones shaken or prodded
    from the pronged tree with whiplash branches.
Their kiwi-green jackets were putty-soft.
    Inside, corrugated as testicles,
hard nuts to crack. Father would not assist,
    so alone she gathered the baskets full,
carried them to the basement to dry out.
    Throughout December the stark hammer blows
echoing inside the house made us wince—
    Thunk! and Thunk! and Thunk! as she split
                    black nuts
sacrificed upon a cement block. Days
    it took to crack the lot, and then for days
she worked with a nutpick to retrieve the white
    meat from each hull, like flesh from a lobster.
The rooms smelled acrid, sharp—good scent of walnut.
    Finally she showed a Tupperware bowl full.
Christmas, tollhouse cookies, applesauce cakes
    blazoned her walnuts. Father ate the most.
Me, she taught the sweet result of labor,
    and the importance of a direct hit.

Piano Lessons

(for Lilian Beaulieu Hopkins)

The best times came when we exchanged places
       and she sat before the keyboard, hands poised,
then tore into "Soaring," "Carnival," or
       "The Waldstein." Former pupil of Gebhardt,
fellow pupil with Bernstein, she mumbled
       apologies if she fumbled a trill,
an arpeggio. No apologies
       needed—she filled that long rectangular
room with the first live classical music
       I'd heard. Rubenstein could not have thrilled me
more. As her fingers flew across the grand,
       she was transported to Back Bay Boston
of her girlhood, I was transported to
       any place but where I had to grow up.

Shyest boy in the class, he
creates a landscape of breath-
taking originality: green sky,
lilac grass, lemon tree trunks,
black leaves. Horses are orange,
cows are pink, zanily they dance
together across a purple pasture,
ears long as jackrabbits'
(if jackrabbits were big as cows).
A sun brown as a nut smiles down.

Other children gather around,
admire the shy boy's world.
"Look! Look! and Look!" they cry.
Until the teacher comes to see,
to frown. "Richard!" she scolds,
"The sky is not green, grass is
green. The sun is not brown,
cows are brown." She removes it,
returns with a blank sheet. "Now,
draw the world as it really is."

I'm not the lucky type, I always say,
I never won a thing in my life. But
that's not quite true. Once, young,
I won something at a Saturday matinee
at Schine's Waller Theater in Laurel,
Delaware. Kids packed the theater for
the drawing, popcorn littered the floor.
Noisily we sat through previews
of coming attractions, newsreels, cartoons,
a Hopalong Cassidy, and a Gene Autry.

Finally the house lights came up
and Mr. Kopf, the theater manager,
ambled onstage, blinking like an owl
behind wire-rim spectacles. He wore
white-buck shoes and chewed gum.
Now, he announced, now was the moment
we all had been waiting for. Now
he would produce a slip of paper
from the goldfish bowl and proclaim
the winner of the brand-new Schwinn

bicycle. From the wings he wheeled
it onstage. It stood propped
on its kickstand: shiny, coveted,
and red. I didn't have a bike;
at twelve I was the only kid I knew
who didn't. Was our family too large,
too poor? Hadn't I begged hard enough?
I don't know. But I remember imagining
me Schwinning my way about town,
a red blur, happy as a boy can be.

Mr. Kopf drew the piece of paper.
It had Billy Prettyman's name on it.
(Billy was the town dentist's son.
An only child, he had two bicycles.)
Kids began to hiss and boo. Billy
didn't mind. He ran down the aisle,
up carpeted stairs to claim what he
believed he deserved. (I never knew
what he did with his other two bikes.
Kept them, I assume—a collection.)

Then Mr. Kopf looked mischievous,
announced the drawing wasn't over.
There was to be a Consolation Prize.
From the wings he produced a sack
of potatoes. Everyone laughed, but
not so hard as when my name was called.
I walked down that aisle as if toward
the guillotine. When he handed me
"the prize," laughter began again.
From orchestra to balcony, derision.

Then I carried that hateful sack home.
It grew heavier with every block,
the potatoes reeked of dirt. I thought
of Jesus writhing on the tree
while Barabbas was set free. I considered
throwing the sack away. But my parents
would hear that I had "won," and I knew
that we could use those potatoes. Sunday
Mother cooked some in an Irish stew.
It stuck to the roof of my mouth like glue.

To make a soapbox racing car
no longer was the project.
What father or Cub Scout son
could even find a wooden soapbox
those postmodern days of 1977?

Instead, each boy was handed
a rectangular block of wood
and four axled plastic wheels,
told to return next week
with a completed model rally car.

Fathers were allowed to help.
But the depths of my incompetence,
naivete, were unparalleled.
I hacked and stabbed and chiseled
at that hard block with penknife;

other fathers masterfully power-
sawed, fretsawed, powersanded,
ultra-streamlined, supersmoothed.
Ours resisted taking shape—
a jalopy painted by Grandma Moses.

The hoots that greeted him when
he presented that homely thing!
He was unconsoled when, democratic,
the scoutmasters raced it anyway.
Downhill it came in a cool third.

(I'd buried a lead sinker in the nose.)
That qualified it and him to go on
to regional racing competition.
But other fathers said its appearance
would be "an embarrassment to the Pack."

The next assignment was to make a kite.
No powertools needed for that. Taking
shelf paper and two wooden sticks
and a good horsehoof glue, I made
a kite that flew and flew and flew—

It seemed weightless and designed
to belly big against March skies!
Together we'd painted the sun's
smiling face on its fragile facade,
and it beamed down like a god.

Everyone admired it as it sailed above
the Saturday town, five-foot tail
trailing bows of cellophane. My son
held the line in both small hands
and felt the flailing tug of love.

cries for days in rampant display,
lamenting the loss of his mate,

who strangled on a lead weight
affixed to abandoned fishing line,

circles the mirror lake, searching
for one his constant heart dreads

he will not find. Pieces of bread
are tossed by villagers come to observe.

For weeks he will not eat,
filled only with his trumpeting.

Signs are posted banning anything
that would further trash the waters,

to no avail. Morning proclaims
a piece of junk floating there—

black, unswanlike, and unaware.

Souvenirs

Collected on our kitchen windowsill,
they resemble an international convocation.

The German pipecleaner chimneysweep,
complete with ladder and stovepipe hat.

A miniature coffee cup whose shamrocks spell
"Souvenir of Ireland," as if you couldn't tell.

Two porous turquoise tiles from a kiln
in Spain. A soap, pressed like fresh butter

to display a Dutch windmill. The china Siamese
cat, straight from the jungles of California . . .

A motley crew, not worth more than a dollar
or two, talismen from lands we imagined

exotic, inexhaustible. Their function was
to make times past new. Today they look

ordinary, gather dust, tell us life is much the same
everywhere. We can't escape where we are.

I

Blue and Gold Poem

Feeling like a hospital intern,
    I carry a stainless steel bowl
across the lawn to harvest the sun-
    flower seeds. For months those flowers
stretched, swayed, nodded, slumbered,
    posturing against an Aegean blue
garage. Their yellow and gold
    contrasted with that blue, composing
their own version of van Gogh.
    Early fall. All the cardinals
cheep-cheep-cheep, making cheap shots,
    groundfeeders in hopes of a handout.
The sky, less blue than the garage,
    is bored with being sky blue so long.
As I begin to scrape sunflower seeds
    with bare fingers, they ping, pang,
and pong into the metal bowl,
    an aria from Puccini—*Turandot.*
The bowl fills, soon the cardinals will,
    and I shall return to the house
to start the season's first fire,
    and dream of sunflowers in October.

II

Bittersweet

All summer long it lightly rained in the leaves,
    gypsy moth caterpillars working
terrible mandibles, stripping all our trees.
    Only the apple stood refulgent, green.
But up close, it was an articulation of bittersweet,
    a tent of woody vines pitched over bare branches,
a nest of serpents struggling toward the light.
    This apple would bear no apples, another fruit—
orange berries, shocking scarlet flesh and root.
    Bittersweet spreads fast as kudzu,
tendrils restless as moths. Stubby plants,
    they exceed themselves by climbing upon
their neighbors' backs. It was some summer
    in our nude yard, but a false face, camouflage.

Like unrequited love, too much hugging smothers.
With pleasure and pain I ripped the bittersweet
down.

III

Rue

You bought that shrub simply out of pity—
its odd and twisted, yellow-fringed flowers
so hideous, whoever else would buy it?

The teardrop blue leaves smell musty and sharp.
You were cautioned you could contract a rash
just by handling or brushing against them.

Could there ever be a plant less charming?
In literature it symbolizes
repentance: "With rue my heart is laden . . ."

In mythology, it's the only thing
on earth the monster Basilisk could not
wither with one long reptilian glance.

Now all winter, in your dead garden, rue
flourishes, vibrant green, through snow, ice:
tough, tenacious, working hard to be loved.

IV

Persimmons

The first fruit tree
to bear on our acre,
the persimmon tempted,
inexorable orange plums.
I was forewarned
at an early age,
wouldn't wait for
first frost to soften,
transform them,
render them edible.
Like Adam, I was
bidden, succumbed.
One taste is all
it took: That tart,
astringent taste
puckered my mouth

like alum—roof afire,
orifice lined with fur.
I spit: threw the hateful
persimmons away.
Yet so it seems to be
with me. Importunate,
impetuous, taking
cherries before girls
were eager, landing
a plum of a job
in the Big Apple
while quite green,
clamoring to be
the Top Banana,
expecting fruits
of my labor before
they'd been earned.
When will I learn
to wait for time
to ripen everything,
as it ripens
the succulence
of persimmons, hanging
in the chill weather?

v

Forsythia

Wordsworth can have his daffodils.
The host of spring I welcome most
is forsythia. No low-to-the-ground
flower bowing and scraping in the wind;
burning bush, bower of blossoming,
shower of gold, fountains of petals
spraying parabolas into innocent air.
Bernini would have approved.

Impatient for their coming,
you can break branches and force
their festivity unnaturally early.
All that they ask is a little tap water,
not even a place in the sun. Twigs
soaked long enough will produce
hairy roots. Plant these sticks,
a bush will bloom. Forsythia spreads.

Yellow blossoms appear along stems
before green leaves—sufficient oddity.
What of forcing? Against nature?
Ritual for an unready virgin?
Marrow sucked from a kitten's bones?
There is a season for all things.
Beauty should be consummate unfurling.
Let altars remain bare in a cold spring.

AMERICAN
ELEGIES

(Charles Ives, 1874–1954)

"Bringing in the Sheaves"
         sashaying in counterpoint
to "Turkey in the Straw"?—

Just maybe innovation
         in Yankee music commenced
when George Ives, organist,

cornetist, bandsman, father
         of Charles, fiendishly arranged
one ordinary afternoon

for two bands to march
         through Danbury, Connecticut,
from opposite directions,

playing different tunes
         in different keys.
Like a town meeting, every man

for himself, "Old Black Joe"
         competing with "Yankee Doodle
Dandy," "Columbia, Gem

of the Ocean" tangling with
         "Where, Oh Where, are
the Pea-Green Freshmen"?

Brightly blared the brass!
         Tremulous were the reeds!
Raucous rose the chord clusters.

An ear-splitting, contrapuntal
         free-for-all. Dissonance
and cacophony. As sounds

gnashed and clashed,
         townspeople held ears. But
George's son, Charles, grinned:

Those polytonal disharmonies,
        those unities of disunities,
were they the start of Charles's

own iconoclastic American music?
        Born in chaos, vitalized
by chaos, out of chaos—

Music of a new order.

Fish heads fertilized cornfields.
Flower petals made potpourri.
Rags became patchwork quilts.
Cigar boxes served as canvasses.
The crime was not to throw something
away. The crime was to be unable
to think of something to make of it.

"Drive Friendly"

(Texas interstate road sign)

How to accomplish this latest admonition
from the Texas Department of Public Safety?
Will I become a better driver if I take one
or both hands off the wheel and wave gaily
at approaching automobiles? Or blink my lights?

Or toot the horn in amicable fashion
when passing through sleeping neighborhoods?
To operate a motor vehicle deep in this part
of Texas, do I need a ten-gallon hat
to tip at every woman driver?

I don't observe my fellow Texans driving
especially friendly, especially that S.O.B.
in the black Porsche convertible,
cutting me off in the middle lane.
Or the pickup who took away my right-of-way.

The Jeep behind me never dims its high beams.
The recreational vehicle up ahead zigs
and zags between lanes like a water beetle.
What gives them the license to drive
so unfriendly? Can't they read?

Native Texans know "Drive Friendly"
is merely the flip side of a warning:
In inclement weather it reads,
"Watch for Ice on Bridge"—
a sign giving Friendly the cold shoulder.

I envision a day when everyone will
Drive Friendly. Drivers will fling flowers
from open windows, blossoms sailing
from car to car in convivial exchange.
Highways will be strewn like Palm Sunday.

Or perhaps they fling confetti,
toilet paper fluttering down gaily—
even a trip to the Stop 'n' Shop
will become a ticker-tape parade,
every citizen a returning astronaut.

Balloons will hang like rubber clouds
over the beltways. Banners will festoon
traffic signals. Every driver will blow
kisses from car to car like Miss America,
and it will be friendly, friendly, friendly.

Paradise

(for Gloria and Daniel Stern)

      was living in Beverly Hills—
pseudo-Spanish adobe, swimming pool,
Mexican maid, jacuzzi whirl.
They reached out, picked avocados
off their trees. Odor of orange blossom,
flame of bougainvillea, silver Mercedes
and black Porsche ticked in their drive.
Every morning she rose, drew heavy
damask drapes, and cried:
"Another goddamn perfect day!"
Living in the Garden of Eden,
they wanted out.

      Back in Manhattan,
she jokes, "We traded Beverly Hills
for Beverly Sills, and she retired."
But mornings she rises expectantly,
a Christmas child, opens shutters
to sallow skies, smirched snows,
leaden rain which scribbles down,
meager autumn leaves, August indignities.
Once in winter the postman creaks
through drifts to vocalize,
"Ain't this the pits?" "No,"
she sighs, "Paradise."

When, one by one, the underpants,
tee shirts, handkerchiefs are sorted,
folded, put in appropriate
drawers, the single socks remain

to be reckoned with: maiden aunts,
bachelor uncles, abandoned
in the wicker laundry basket.
They cry out to be paired, scolded,

turned inside out with a soul mate.
Where do they wander, the lost socks?
To some black hole in the Whirlpool?
Do they transcend permanent press,

cartwheel through the starry vortex,
land on a distant stone altar
where barren women pray for birth?
Do new mates wait on a new plane?

Surely you put them in the wash
like animals in the Ark, two
by two. But invariably
a stray emerges, asunder.

Silk or cotton, polyester
or wool, they are your second skin—
like a panther's pelt which kings wore
casually knotted round their waists.

Just when you feel complacent, one
goes down for the count, is missing
in action, prodigal son, lost
knowledge. Learn to count on nothing.

A Little Elegy for Howard Moss

(1922–1987)

Howard, you died so many different deaths.
Once an ordinary mosquito bite
became, in your eyes, sign of Lyme Disease.
In the East, it was all the rage that year.
An occasional headache? A tumor
big as an avocado on the brain.
Your prickly heat? The beginning of AIDS.
You name it, you thought you had it in spades.

So when you fled your classes at midterm,
leaving Houston to see your New York internist,
saying, "I feel strange," we said, "That's Howard!"
Except this time symptoms were genuine.
You had real pneumonia, real phlebitis,
a real spot on your lungs and a real heart
attack that turned you to cement late one night.
Even hypochondriacs have real illnesses.

I miss your astringent humor, Old Sport,
your understating every blessed thing
except your health—that topic was sacred.
And how your mind managed to qualify:
"X is quite masterful in what he does;
but what *is* it he does?" It took the breath.
Now your breath's taken, since last fall shut down,
I still resist the urge to telephone.

That's perhaps the biggest vacuum I feel,
knowing I can't pick up the phone to dish
about this one and that—real people
the creations that fascinated you most.
Yet for all your knowledge of character,
you seemed unaware of the role you played—
fawning of would-be poet sycophants,
dislike of thousands of rejectees, un-
discerned. You died not knowing who you were.

(John I. H. Baur, 1909–1987)

1.

Years ago you'd seen on the TV
a commercial for inexpensive cremation.
You signed on. After your death,
your family found the run-down place
in White Plains, a factory of sorts.
A rumpled old man ushered them through.
One daughter asked to view the body
alone. She found you on a table
in a box of the flimsiest wood—
not even pine. It buckled and bowed
like an orange crate. Inside,
you looked none the worse for wear.

But that room was bare and shabby,
the only ornament a reproduction
of a ghastly painting—angels dancing
in a grotto—directly over the box.
It's a wonder you didn't roll,
you who helped set standards of an age.
Your daughter rectified. Reaching
into her bag, she took out some Magic
Markers, began to draw: flowers,
butterflies, cats, dogs, clouds,
rainbows appeared on that humbling box.
Done, she summoned the family in.

2.

It was your independence I admired,
that and your absolute honesty.
Like the time I had you to the house
to apprise my latest proud possession—
a painting by an obscure Englishman
whose work I admired, bought sight unseen
through an auctioneer's catalog.
And when I brought that picture out
and held it before your level gaze,
you took one look, nodded, and declared,
"Perfectly dreadful!" Instead of separating,
you cemented our friendship, fast.

3.
Nothing could pin you down.
Not the tractor pushing snow
which tipped with you on it,
trapping you underneath, pelvis
broken, age seventy-three.
When you didn't come in for supper,
your wife investigated.
You could have frozen to death.
Instead, you navigated a walker
in what seemed like weeks.

Not the jam-packed bookcase
in your city pad, which tipped
when you tried to extricate
a Trollope novel tightly wedged
on that topmost shelf.
With quick reflexes you held
the falling case back with one leg
while leaping aside. A bruise
or two is all you got from that,
cheating a literary way to go.

4.
Nothing could pin you down,
I thought, unaware of the clogged
left ventricle. You popped nitro-
glycerine daily, after climbing
the train platform. No one saw.
Seventy-eight now, you left your coat
on the train, raced back, found it,
carried it through the station,
panting, were struck to the floor.
Strangers got you to Bellevue.

The doctors couldn't pin you down
to agree to a bypass operation:
"I'll *think* about it," you said,
hooked to five individual monitors.
At midnight the medico on duty
observed all five screens black
out simultaneously. Five never go
at once. He reported a power failure.
There was one, inside you. You did it.
Another feat of absolute will:

Nothing was going to pin you down.
Rather than live a diminished life,
I think you took your exit with grace,
opted for minimum loss of face.
If you couldn't cross-country ski,
couldn't jog around the reservoir,
couldn't come and go to the city,
couldn't garden—then to hell with it!
(Your last aesthetic pronouncement.)
Nothing was going to pin you down.

Flower Fires

(To the Memory of Muriel Rukeyser, 1913–1980)

I

"The flowers are on fire!"
our dinner guest cried.
I leapt to pull the bouquet
away from the candle's dancing
flame. It licked purple,
white, and red anemones as one
cat affectionately licks another.
A song flew out of the flowers
as night flies out of day.
The room filled with the odor.
Scored blossoms, broken promises.

II

Decades earlier my mother,
a young girl, attended
a Hallowe'en party
costumed as a flower:
blouse and skirt furled
with yellow cheesecloth
petals sewn by Grandmother.
When she paraded past
the open jack-o'-lantern,
Mother's petals trailed
the lit candle, burst
into blossoms of fire.
Frantically she raced
around the attic room,
body half in flame,
until a quick adult
rolled her in a blanket,
drove her home before
refreshments were served.

III

One noon in April, nineteen fifty-eight,
the Museum of Modern Art in Manhattan,
one of Monet's *Waterlilies* was destroyed.
Flames ate the dry canvas, ate cool pads
and buds, blossoms and stems, roots and mud

and water, all curling into blisters,
a burning pool, cool currents flowing
into hot fire, thirsting, drinking in
creamy dewy flowers, waterlilies drinking
dark instead of day, forced not into bloom
but oblivion, a phoenix bursting out
of the bushes, singing as it soars upward
toward the great domed bell of noon.

IV

There are many Monet *Waterlilies*.
I have been surrounded by them
in the Musée de l'Orangerie.
But that is the one I miss,
waterlilies in Manhattan
of my young manhood, just as I miss
fiery Muriel, who first wrote
of the phenomenon of waterlily fire.
Before she died her ample body dwindled,
a flame gasping in the crosscurrent,
going, going, gone. Ashes on a hearth,
ashes in an urn. Her poems still burn.

Acknowledgments

Some of these poems first appeared, sometimes in different form, in the following periodicals and anthologies:

"Drive Friendly," "Elegy for an Art Critic," and "Flower Fires": *Borderlands: Texas Poetry Review*
"Face to Face," "In Concert," "The Hole," and "Rue": *Boulevard*
"Bittersweet" and "Genius": *Chelsea*
"The Married Man": *Choice*
"Avant-Garde Music Comes to America," "Baltimore & Ohio R.R.," "Ghost Story," "A Little Elegy for Howard Moss," "Scouting Days," "The Stone Crab," and "Walnuts": *Hudson Review*
"Easy Street": *Illinois Review*
"The Cutting" and "Despair": *Lips*
"The Matched Pair" and "Forsythia": *Manhattan Poetry Review*
"Happiness": *Mudfish*
"Black Swan at Schloss Benrath": *New Criterion*
"Hardwood": *New Republic*
"After the Fact: To Ted Bundy" and "Breakdown Lane": *Ontario Review*
"On a Drawing by Glen Baxter": *Paris Review*
"Letter from the Country," "Suburban Interior," and "Wish You Were Here": *Poetry*
"The Stone Crab": *Pushcart Prize Anthology*
"The Carving": *Southern Review*
"On Finding a Former Lover Cut All Dedications to Me from Her Selected Poems" and "Whereabouts": *Western Humanities Review*

Some poems appeared in a chapbook, *Face to Face* (Houston: Wings Press, 1993).
The author wishes to thank the MacDowell Colony for generous support which made the writing of some of these poems possible.

Some Other Books by Robert Phillips

Poetry
Inner Weather, 1966
The Pregnant Man, 1978
Running on Empty, 1981
Personal Accounts: New & Selected Poems, 1986
The Wounded Angel (limited edition, with etchings by
 DeLoss McGraw), 1986
Face to Face (chapbook), 1993

Fiction
The Land of Lost Content, 1970
Public Landing Revisited, 1992

Criticism
Aspects of Alice (editor), 1971
The Confessional Poets, 1973
Denton Welch, 1974
William Goyen, 1979

Poetry Titles in the Series

John Hollander, *"Blue Wine" and Other Poems*
Robert Pack, *Waking to My Name: New and Selected Poems*
Philip Dacey, *The Boy under the Bed*
Wyatt Prunty, *The Times Between*
Barry Spacks, *Spacks Street: New and Selected Poems*
Gibbons Ruark, *Keeping Company*
David St. John, *Hush*
Wyatt Prunty, *What Women Know, What Men Believe*
Adrien Stoutenberg, *Land of Superior Mirages: New and Selected Poems*
John Hollander, *In Time and Place*
Charles Martin, *Steal the Bacon*
John Bricuth, *The Heisenberg Variations*
Tom Disch, *Yes, Let's: New and Selected Poems*
Wyatt Prunty, *Balance as Belief*
Tom Disch, *Dark Verses and Light*
Thomas Carper, *Fiddle Lane*
Emily Grosholz, *Eden*
X. J. Kennedy, *Dark Horses*
Wyatt Prunty, *The Run of the House*
Robert Phillips, *Breakdown Lane*

Library of Congress Cataloging-in-Publication Data

Phillips, Robert S.
  Breakdown lane / by Robert Phillips.
        p.   cm. — (Johns Hopkins, poetry and fiction)
  ISBN 0-8018-4854-7 (acid-free paper). — ISBN 0-8018-4855-5 (pbk. :
acid-free paper)
  I. Title.   II. Series.
PS3566.H5B7   1994
811'.54—dc20   93-43813